HOLYWELL C.E.(C.) SCHOOL,
NEEDINGWORTH, HUNTINGDON
CAMBS. PE17 3TR.

£1.29

D1439144

Osbert
and
Lucy

words and pictures by
Ronald Ferns

Hutchinson

London Melbourne Auckland Johannesburg

Copyright © Ronald Ferns 1988

All rights reserved

First published in Great Britain in 1988 by Hutchinson Children's Books
An imprint of Century Hutchinson Ltd
Brookmount House, 62-65 Chandos Place
Covent Garden, London WC2N 4NW

Century Hutchinson Australia (Pty) Ltd
16-22 Church Street, Hawthorn, Melbourne, Victoria 3122

Century Hutchinson New Zealand Limited
32-34 View Road, PO Box 40-086, Glenfield, Auckland 10

Century Hutchinson South Africa (Pty) Ltd
PO Box 337, Bergvlei 2012, South Africa

Designed by ACE Limited

Set in Century Old Style Roman by The Graphic Unit, London

Printed and bound in Portugal

British Library Cataloguing in Publication Data
Ferns, Ronald
Osbert and Lucy.
I. Title
823′.914[J]

ISBN 0-09-173595-5

Somewhere in a small town there was a certain house.
Mr and Mrs Good lived there with their dog, Osbert
Good. In the back garden there was a little hutch where
lived a white rabbit, named Lucy.

Osbert and Lucy were good friends.

Osbert Good was a very nice dog, except for one thing: he liked to listen at doorways. One day he overheard three words that made him very alarmed. They were:
    'delicious,
    rabbit', and
    'dinner'.
    This could only mean one thing. No! They couldn't, they mustn't eat his friend Lucy.

Osbert hurried into the garden to tell Lucy what he had
overheard. Lucy didn't like the idea of becoming dinner
for Mr and Mrs Good. But Osbert had a plan. They
would run away together.

In the middle of the night, Osbert opened the door to
Lucy's hutch and out she hopped. She put some lettuce
leaves in a tiny bag. Osbert took with him a bone and an
umbrella.

They set off together into the night. Although Osbert walked slowly, Lucy had to hop very quickly to keep up.

The rain fell in big drops, making large puddles on the pavement. 'Oh, what shall we do! Where shall we go!' wailed Lucy.

'Everything will be all right, as long as we stay together,' said Osbert.

Soon they came to an empty house. There was a sign
outside saying:
   'FOR SALE'.
   'Let's shelter here for a while,' said Osbert.

He shook the raindrops from his umbrella while Lucy
held the bags of food.

As Lucy leant against the door, it began to open. Cautiously, the two friends crept inside and bravely climbed the stairs.

'No one will find us here,' said Lucy, beginning to feel
better. They were both tired and hungry. Lucy nibbled
her lettuce leaves and Osbert gnawed his bone. Soon
they were both fast asleep.

They woke up as the dawn sunshine shone through the dusty window. Osbert and Lucy peered out together. This is what they saw:

There was a neat garden with flower beds.
There was a vegetable patch.
There were some fruit bushes.
And beyond the gate there was a leafy wood.

They raced downstairs. The back door was locked, but at the bottom they found a cat flap. Lucy slipped through easily. Osbert found it rather difficult, but he squeezed and he huffed and he pushed and he puffed and, eventually, he found himself outside.

'Oh, it's lovely,' cried Lucy, looking round the garden.
She was soon enjoying a fine breakfast of tender lettuce
leaves and fresh carrots.

Poor Osbert wandered around hoping he could find
something to eat. If only he were a vegetarian, too.

Then he noticed a packet near the wall. Inside were sandwiches: corned beef, cheese and jam. He was so hungry and in such a hurry to eat that he dropped most of the slices of bread.

Birds flew down from the trees and snapped up the bread. Ants scurried from the cracks in the path and carried the jammy bits away to eat at home.

Soon everything was gone.

Time passed. Lucy seemed to love life in the garden.
She found plenty of carrots and lettuce leaves, but poor
Osbert could find nothing at all to eat.

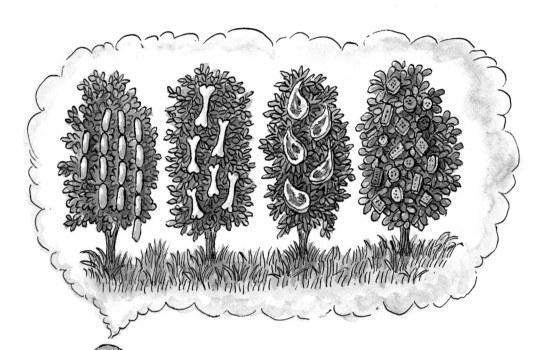

He sat down in a corner of the garden and wished, 'If only sausages, bones, lamb chops and biscuits grew on trees.' But they didn't.

Osbert thought about his comfortable home, his regular meals and his basket. Then he thought about his favourite ball and his collection of squeaky toys. He became very sad and great big tears rolled down his nose. 'Rabbits can live in the wild,' he said, sadly. 'But dogs need a home, and a bone, and a warm, dry basket.'

He wandered off to find Lucy. She was holding hands with another rabbit. 'This is Henry,' she explained. 'He came over from the wood where he lives. He has asked me to marry him, and I feel inclined to accept. But what will you do, Osbert?'

'Congratulations!' said Osbert. 'Oh, I do hope you'll be happy. Please don't worry about me, I'll go back home. After all, I don't think they'll eat *me* for dinner.'

So Lucy and Henry were married.

When Osbert reached home again, Mr and Mrs Good
were very pleased to see him.

'How clever of Osbert to find our lost umbrella,' they said. 'What a pity he couldn't find Lucy as well.'

Later that same day, Osbert Good was listening at the
door again. This time he heard the words:
    'delicious,
    dinner,'
  and 'now – the jelly'.

Mrs Good walked out from the kitchen carrying a large wobbly pink jelly rabbit! Osbert felt rather silly. So they hadn't meant to eat Lucy after all! Still, he was glad he hadn't taken any chances, for . . .

now he could visit Lucy and Henry in the wood. They have a very large family with many children, a number of grand-children and several great-grand-children.

And he knows that although he needs a home and a
bone and a dry basket, Lucy is much better off where
she is.